I AM

edited and illustrated by
Angeli R. Rasbury

Revolution Begins with Me Press

Published by Angeli R. Rasbury, Revolution Begins with Me Press
www.angelirasbury.com
angelirasbury@gmail.com

To purchase: email angelirasbury@gmail.com
 To discuss a reading, program or workshop, email angelirasbury@gmail.com.

Printed in the USA
Book and cover design by Angeli R. Rasbury

This book is dedicated to the children and teens
who have particpated in the writing workshops
I have offered and facilitated over the years and
to children and teens who write poetry and who love
writing and art. You inspire me.

Introduction

I Am gives voice to young Black writers. It gives voice to Black community and culture and keeps them alive. I Am is in the tradition of Who Look at Me, June Jordan's first book of poetry, and Ridin' the Moon in Texas: Word Paintings by Ntozake Shange. Like June Jordan did over the years, I facilitate writing workshops and encourage the children and teens to write freely. I also facilitate exploration of poets and writers such as June Jordan, Nikki Giovanni, Lucille Clifton, Ntozake Shange, Gwendolyn Brooks, and Sonia Sanchez. I use music and art to inspire the children and teens and to share the contributions and legacy of Black musicians and artists like Romare Bearden and Nina Simone. The poems and prose collected in I Am were inspired by some of my photographs and paintings with the exception of "In the Park". "In the Park" was inspired by the title of a book See the Music Hear the Dance: Rethinking African Art at the Baltimore Museum of Art edited by Frederick John Lamp. The photographs and paintings inspiring Girl in Yellow Dress and the other collected writing and the painting inspired by "In the Park" have been reproduced in these pages. The writing adds colors, details and beauty to the art. Inspired by the young writers' voices, we can imagine and build a better community, a better tomorrow.

Angeli R. Rasbury
Brooklyn, NY
May 2012

Yellow Dress
Najaya Royal

It seems like the sun loves my dress
cuz it seems like it only shines on me
I love how the wind
makes my yellow dress
flow to my steps
Walking bare foot
on the slightly wet grass
I feel like I am in heaven
So relaxed
A few hours later the
time has come
The sun is setting
It went from bright yellow to the
yellowish, orange shade of my dress
then to lavender
I stand out and it's dark
I stand out and watch the moon rise
It seems it is within
arm's reach
As the stars come into sight
I start to walk home
and I can't wait
till tomorrow.

I Am
Ardelle Stowe

I am listening to my mama play jazz. I try to tap dance shoeless in my little yellow dress. I try to make myself look cute and hope to be noticed. I feel so different in a white world. I feel comforted because I know what Mama says. "Your character is more beautiful than your skin."

I am called up on stage to dance. The audience stares at me like I am tiny and they are looking for me.

I dance. I impress Mama and myself. I want to be a dancer when I grow up. Mama says, Be original.

Now I am all grown up, I am conducting my very own poetry class. There are days I feel so bad that I did not accomplish what I wanted to do when I was younger. There are days I wish I could have accomplished my dream. But Mama helped me to learn that dancing is not the only way I can express myself.

The first time I came to the library, I was asked my name.

"Angeli," I replied.

Now, I am showing my little poets what I looked like when I was younger.

Girl in Yellow Dress
Adedayo Abimbola

Angeli is in her yellow dress dancing and practicing in her room.

"Angeli, are you ready?"

"No Mama! I'm still practicing." I close my eyes. I imagine all the people that will be there. Even famous people. Oh the misery. "What will I do?" I don't want to go. Should I? Oh the fun! Dancing is my passion. I still remember my first talent show. I'm still amazed I won first place. It was so frightening. Dancing is too good to give up. I'm going. I am brave, talented and amazing.

Dad called. "Angeli, are you finished?"

"Yes!" I yelled.

From our home outside Los Angeles we head to Hollywood. During the drive I think about all the practicing. I am so dressed up and ready. I got what it takes. I close my eyes and think of faithfulness. Mom and dad encourage me to follow my dreams.

Finally we arrive. What a huge place.

From behind the curtain I hear my name. I go out on stage ready to do my thing. I signal the DJ. Here I go.

I dance to pop, jazz, and more. Next thing you know people are shouting, "Encore." I dance and dance.

Outside after the show someone shouts, "What is your name?"

"Just call me Angeli."

Next thing you know people are shouting, "Angeli."

I smile. I got an award, a scholarship and a standing ovation.

New Baby
Eva Taylor

I am at the beach
I want to share my feelings with God in the open water
I am happy
I can hear children screaming and laughing
I am joyful
I get to lay out my towel and feel the lump of sand piles under it
I am sad
People drown and get swiped away in the ocean
And that's the end of their life
I feel the windy breeze lift my hair in the air
I feel the baby next to me playing with gold and power
And most importantly with love
And passion
I go to the water's edge
I dig and dig and find gold and give it to the baby

Mr. Red and the Pesky Rabbit
Jasmine Williams

Once in a garden, there was a pesky rabbit. It was always eating Mr. Red's flowers. One day Mr. Red was so mad, he screamed at the top of his lungs. His friends heard him and came running.

When they got to him, they asked, "Are you okay?"

He said, "I'm okay but that rabbit is damaging my garden!"

Then his friend said, "It's okay. We know how to get rid of it."

Then his friend got drums and started to play. Soon Mr. Red began to play along.

In the Park
DaShanae Hardy

Sitting in the park under
the biggest apple tree
dreamy clouds
big round yellow sun
seeing music notes to "No One"
my favorite Alicia Keys' song
squiggly lines going side to side
in black and white
in the
baby blue sky

I can't hear the dance
but I can see
the dance
beautiful African American women
wearing colorful African skirts
dancing to my favorite song
turning and twisting
their bodies from
side to side
moving across the dance floor
sweat coming down their faces

I can't smell love
but I see it
and hear it
Little kids helping elderly women across Fulton Street
Children being nice
to one another
saying, "You're a great friend.
You're the notes to my music"
in the big Brooklyn park.

The Ocean
Keanu Stowe

Even the slave
ship loves it
but when it
comes to slaves
on a ship the
ocean hesitates
to move.
The crew
has to whip the
ocean to get a
move on.

One day the
drummer in Harlem
wearing a dashiki
sits on his stoop.
His ears perk up.
He hears wonderful
sounds and thinks,
What a wonderful
ocean it is. I should
have a meeting with
it tomorrow at dawn.

That night the drummer thinks
about what to say.
Should I say,
Good afternoon ocean
or maybe even say,
Hello generous?
Then he decides.
I'll play the drums to the tune
of my heart.

The Cotton Girl
Jaya Samuel

A little girl picking cotton
Isn't that sad?
It makes me depressed and mad
And some white people glad
Look at her
She works oh so hard
She needs to hold her guard
Be strong
Crack, crack, crack
Goes the bad black back
Of the poor slave
Out in the sun all day
Must make her tired in many ways
If she wants to escape
She needs to face the people
Of hate
If she dies
She will be free
Of shattering lies
Just keep picking that cotton
And one day you will
Set yourself free.

"The times I hated most was pickin' cotton when the frost was on the bolls. My hands git sore and crack open and bleed."--Mary Reynolds, Slave Narrative from the Federal Writers' Project, 1936-1938

My Soil
Dyqwai Rice

I watch people work
and break their backs
while whites call them countless hacks
slave masters beat their backs
and the sound is like one thousand slaps
will torture stop? Perhaps
they will die from brutal snaps
They live in cabins like hens or chickens
In the day they just keep picking
eat hog maws and chitlins
watching masters eat like kings
They rely on hope and faith, but
a fling of the machete
will make them break down
On their hands
their tears water
my soil
nourishing the cotton.

Trees
Aliah Gilkes

Trees
My safety
Tower and fortress
My rock, salvation
The Lord, my God

Trees
A place of safety
In times of trouble
Supports and protects
Jehovah-Shaloam

Trees
The center of everything
A covering and shield at all times
My provider and the branch
Jehovah-Shammah

Trees
Supporter
Protector
Shield
The Lord, my God

In the night they came
Ardelle Stowe

In the dead of night they came
and asked for clothes and food
and to spend the night.
I don't know the people,
but I sure do know
the leader.
It is Harriet Tubman
standing before me in flesh and blood.
She's all everybody's been talking about.
She says I can join her
if I want.
Like anybody else who looked up to her
I oblige.
I am like any other slave.
I want to be free
so I join her.
We sleep all day and
travel by night.
It takes forever but finally
Harriet says we left the
boundaries of the south.
We give a silent
cheer and continue our journey.
Most people lose track of time

simply because they just
stop counting the sunrises.
But I know it took
many frightful nights to reach
New York.
I'm ready to begin my
new life as a
free person.

Every great dream begins with a dreamer.   Always remember,
you have within you the strength, the patience,
and the passion to reach for the stars to change the world.

------ Harriet Tubman

Made in the USA
Middletown, DE
17 November 2021